Absolutely Mahvelous

Absolutely Mahvelous

~~~~~~~~~~~~~~~~~~~~

Billy Crystal

with Dick Schaap

G. P. Putnam's Sons • New York

G. P. Putnam's Sons
Publishers Since 1838
200 Madison Avenue
New York, NY 10016

Photographs on pages 2, 43, 47, 73, 76, 77, 78, 79, 114, 120,
123 and 128 courtesy of Mark Sennet; on pages 17, 30,
34–35, 48, 57, 61, 62, 68, 82, 101, 102–103, 108 and 112
courtesy of Mark M. Mullen; on page 12 courtesy of Kevin
Fitzgerald/*Sport*; on page 28 courtesy of Bert Andrews; on
page 99 courtesy of Buddy Morra; on page 98 courtesy of the
Los Angeles Dodgers; and on page 104 courtesy of Peter
Montagna. Photo Graphics on pages 102–103 courtesy of
Bob Pook. All other photographs are from the author's
collection.

Library of Congress Cataloging-in-Publication Data

Crystal, Billy.
  Absolutely mahvelous.
    1. Crystal, Billy. 2. Comedians—United States—
Biography. I. Schaap, Dick, date. II. Title.
PN2287.C686A3   1986   792.7'028'0924 [B]   86-12184
ISBN 0-399-51246-2
Book design by Joe Marc Freedman
Typeset by Fisher Composition Inc.
Printed in the United States of America
1 2 3 4 5 6 7 8 9 10

To my parents,
for allowing me to stay up late
to watch Sid Caesar,
and to Janice,
for allowing the kids to stay up late
to watch me.
With love.

CONTENTS

FOREWORD

My Friend Billy Crystal—He Was Terrific Even Before He Was Marvelous

I didn't know that Billy Crystal was funny. I didn't even know who Billy Crystal was.

All I knew was that I needed a comedian to appear at a banquet I had organized to honor Muhammad Ali in 1975 as *Sport* magazine's Man of the Year. Time was running out, and Robert Klein was busy, and a woman who worked at the William Morris Agency was telling me, "Take Billy. He's marvelous. Trust me."

She was an agent. I didn't trust her.

"What does he do?" I said.

"He does a terrific imitation of Ali," the woman said. "Ali and Howard Cosell. You'll love him."

Reluctantly, I took Billy Crystal. I didn't have much choice. I met him for the first time a few minutes before we sat down to eat. He seemed like a nice, gentle person. He said he had been working as a substitute teacher at a junior high school on Long Island. Sometimes he taught social studies. Sometimes he taught girls' gym. He sat on the dais with Neil Simon and George Plimpton, two great writers, and Melba Moore, a great singer, and Muhammad Ali, the greatest. I was afraid Billy was out of his league.

I was afraid I was out of my league, too. I was the master of ceremonies, and halfway through the program, after Simon and Plimpton were witty, and Moore moving, I said, "And now—one of Muhammad Ali's closest friends!"

Billy Crystal stood up and moved toward the microphone, and Ali looked at me as if I were crazed. He had never seen Billy before. He didn't have the slightest idea who he was.

Billy promptly launched into his Ali-and-Cosell routine.

"Muhammad—may I call you 'Mo'?"
"Sure, Howard, but don't call me Larry or Curly."
"How fast are you, Mo?"
"I'm so fast, Howard, I can turn off the light and jump in the bed and be under the covers before the room gets dark."

Ali fell out of his chair, he was laughing so hard. Billy Crystal was the hit of the evening.

Two lasting friendships began that night—one between Muhammad Ali and Billy Crystal, the other between Billy and me. None of us dreamed that a decade later Billy Crystal would be, at least for the moment, a bigger star than Muhammad Ali.

By the end of 1985, millions of people, it seemed, were doing imitations of Billy Crystal. His "you look mahvelous" had become a better-known phrase than Ali's "float like a butterfly, sting like a bee."

Billy Crystal had become a heavyweight—and a champion.

•   •   •

Since 1975 I have watched Billy Crystal grow, on stage and off, with fascination and admiration. His Ali-and-Cosell routine blossomed into part of a nightclub act that made audiences laugh—and made audiences *feel*. Then he stepped into *Soap,* portraying Jodie, the homosexual, on that adult soap opera, and again he combined wit and warmth. In 1984 he became the best part of *Saturday Night Live.*

He wrote. He performed. He hosted. He was Sammy Davis, and he was an aging black baseball player called Rooster. He was an old Jewish man delivering the weather report, and he was Fernando in his Hideaway. He was Buddy Young, Jr., a stereotypical comic, and he was Penny Lane, a transvestite piano player. He was Ricky, who found everything unbelievable, and he was Willie, who found unbelievable ways to abuse himself. Billy changed faces and voices as easily as costumes. His versatility, his gifts were stunning. He was the hottest thing in town.

We couldn't eat lunch without the waiters, the people at the nearby tables, the bartender and a couple of legitimate drunks telling him, "Dahling, you look mahvelous." He must have gotten sick of hearing himself mimicked, but he tried hard not to show it. He was, almost invariably, gracious, pleased to be recognized and—much rarer—even grateful.

Billy Crystal had zoomed to the peak of a profession that routinely inflates egos the way Ali's jab used to puff up opponents' eyes and distorts reality as inevitably as the pounding of a thousand punches. Too many people in Billy's business start out nice and gentle and then, almost before they know what hit them, wind up self-absorbed, self-indulgent and self-serving. Too many wind up believing they really are marvelous, they really are the greatest.

But Billy Crystal, short and wiry, bright and talented, has managed to slip the punches of fame and wealth and adulation, the old one-two-three. He has remained remarkably true to the person he was a decade ago. He is now a movie star, sharing the lead with Gregory Hines in *Running Scared,* but he is still the husband of Janice, still the father of Jennifer, who is thirteen, and now the father, too, of Lindsay, who is eight. Unlike so many in his field, Billy doesn't just *portray* a good husband and a good father. He *is* a good husband and a good father. He could still teach social studies. He could still teach girls' gym.

Billy and his family live in California, halfway between Beverly Hills and the Pacific

Ocean, in Ronald Reagan's old neighborhood, and I live on the opposite coast, but our paths manage to keep crossing. I introduced Billy to Sugar Ray Leonard when Ray was making a commercial in Los Angeles. I introduced Billy to Joe DiMaggio at a fight in Las Vegas. I introduced Billy to another baseball Hall of Famer, Hank Greenberg, on a tennis court in Beverly Hills.

Billy attended my wedding a few years ago and, in his best Jodie, thanked me for making it possible for him to meet men he had always dreamed of meeting. He came to my birthday party more recently and, in his best Fernando, assured me that I looked marvelous, considering my age.

When we get together, we usually talk about wives and children, the New York Yankees and Mickey Mantle, the New York Knicks and Julius Erving, all Billy's deepest loves. We hardly ever touch the subject most performers love best: We hardly ever talk about him.

Of course in working with Billy on this book, in helping him organize this collection of his words and his worlds, I did, occasionally, have to prod him to explore his background, his development, his technique. The one frustration was the knowledge that Billy's facial expressions and vocal inflections, so much a part of his humor, could not accompany every page.

Otherwise, the collaboration was, as I knew it would be, great fun—traveling with Billy to concerts, watching him prepare, watching him work, watching him recuperate from each two-hour explosion, and watching him still find time and energy to plan and promote *Comic Relief,* the television laughathon conceived to raise money to help the homeless in America. I saw Billy share *Comic Relief* news conferences with Mayor Washington in Chicago and with Robin Williams in New York, and I saw him fly off to Washington to lunch with Whoopi Goldberg and Ted Kennedy.

Billy has come so far since the 1975 banquet for Muhammad Ali was filmed and televised. That was Billy's first appearance on national TV, and he stole the show. Several years later, on one of Billy's HBO comedy specials, Ali made a guest appearance. Ali, in a sense, came to honor Billy. They had come full cycle in less than a decade.

Except that Ali was still Ali, despite his physical and mental bruises, still winking and boasting, and Billy, despite all his success, was still Billy.

The woman at William Morris was right: I love him.

Dick Schaap
New York City
March 1986

"That's me with my main man, Ringo—and I mean that."

ONE

≈≈≈≈≈≈

Hey, Billy, How Do You Get Started in Show Business, Anyway?

How do you get started? What do you do? I mean, are you born nuts and then you tell people about it? Like do you drop your pants and everybody watches and then they give you money? I mean, are you just crazy, and people say, "What are you, a comedian?" and you say yeah? Do you walk into a nightclub and say, "Where's a microphone, I'm a comedian"? Do you get residuals for that? Like do you have to go to school for it, or can you just be a dropout or something? Do you write things down or do you just have them in your brain? How do you do that? Do you bang your head against the wall like a nut and then say, "Made you look, made you look"? I mean, do you just make a lot of stupid noises, and then people say, "God, he's noisy," and then you do it for more people? Like do you hang around the living room of your house and everybody laughs and then you say, "Let's put a sign outside that says NIGHT-CLUB"? How do you do that? Do you show off all the time or do you keep it secret so that nobody will steal your stuff? Do you make crazy faces or do you just look like that? I mean, are you retarded, or are you the village idiot or the town crier, or what? How do you think of these things? Do you tape them or record them or just remember everything? Do you get residuals for that? Like do you just wake up one day and you're a star, or what?

TWO

≈≈≈≈≈≈

A Short Autobiography —I Wish It Were Taller

I got started in show business very young. My mother swears I performed prenatally. She says I got a few laughs on the way to the hospital.

You know, you are unbelieeevuble! You're amazing!

It was the best womb I ever played.

When I got older, five or maybe six, I moved up to the living room. I worked to a tough audience. My relatives. When they came to our house in Long Beach on Long Island, I put on their hats and coats and I imitated them. Their hats and coats were too big for me. They still are. And I still imitate them.

A hundred and eight degrees is not a fever! I was dead for six months and didn't know it, goddamit!

I stood on the coffee table and did impressions. If they liked my act, the relatives put . . .

Shrimp forks?

No. Dimes. The relatives gave me dimes and I put them on my forehead, and when my head was filled up, the show was over. My relatives used to worry about Billy getting a big head. They still do. And I still love it when the audience puts . . .

Mentholated eucalyptus cough drops?

No. Dimes. I still love it when the audience gives me dimes to put on my head.

I was bred for show business. My father's father was an actor. He played Hamlet in Yiddish. Shakespeare was even better in Yiddish than in English, but the people in the front row needed raincoats.

My mother carried on the family tradition. She played Minnie Mouse. In English. She sat inside the Minnie Mouse float in the Macy's Thanksgiving Day parade and sang "I'm Forever Blowing Bubbles." Her career never went further.

21

My father did better in the music business. He managed the Commodore music shop and produced concerts, jazz concerts at the Central Plaza on Second Avenue in Manhattan. He used to take me to the Central Plaza. The musicians called me "Face." I met Billie Holiday when I was five. Miss Billie called me *Mister* Billy. The first blind man I ever saw was W. C. Handy. My father used to bring home jazz musicians at Passover. We had swinging seders. Willie "the Lion" Smith, a great piano player, would say, "That pharaoh better hurry up and let them people go, man, we got a gig."

Can you dig that? I knew that you could.

One of my uncles, Milt Gabler, operated the Commodore recording company, then ran Decca. Bill Haley and the Comets cut "Rock Around the Clock" for him. Billie Holiday did her album, *Strange Fruit,* on the Commodore label, and Sammy Davis, Jr., did his first gold record, "Hey There," for Decca. My uncle is in the Grammy Hall of Fame.

My uncle Bern runs an art gallery in Manhattan, the Washington Irving Gallery. He's about six-foot-four and weighs more than 250 pounds. I was sensational in his coat. He went ashore at Normandy *before* D Day, before the Allied invasion. He was a spy/artist. He drew pictures of the German embankments so our boys would know where the danger was. He once introduced me to his friend Zero Mostel.

My father introduced me to Laurel and Hardy and Ernie Kovacs and Sid Caesar. Not in person. On television. My father had a great ear for comedy as well as for music. He brought home gorilla masks so that my older brothers Joel and Rip and I could be Kovacs's Nairobi Trio. We also played Caesar's Three Haircuts. And Joel and I did our own version of Mel Brooks and Carl Reiner's 2,000-year-old man. We did the 2,000-year-old teenager. They loved it in the living room.

With Joel and Richard in a writing meeting before a show in the living room.

Third-grade class play, 1955. "The role of Ariel in
The Tempest *is wonderfully downplayed by*
Mr. Crystal. He is subtle without being childish."
—*the young Eric Feldman, Long Beach* Gazette

Rip sang. He was good. When he was eighteen, he was singing on *The Kraft Music Hall*. Now he's a television producer. He worked on *The Billy Crystal Comedy Hour* a few years ago. Fernando's Hideaway was his idea. Isn't that what brothers are for?

And I mean that.

Joel came up with a terrific idea, too. He invented the baseball game we played in our backyard when we weren't lip-synching Spike Jones records. We used a Little League bat and a badminton shuttlecock, and we laid out a baseball field, in miniature, to the exact proportions of Yankee Stadium—very short right field, very deep center. Joel, who became an art teacher, made a cutout of a catcher, and that was our backstop. If the pitcher threw the shuttlecock and hit the backstop, it was a strike. We called the game "Bird," even before Mark Fidrych.

We played an eighty-game season, with day games and night games. For night games, we took all my mother's lamps out of the living room and put them on extension cords, spreading them around the field with no shades on so they'd give off a good ballpark glow. We had a whole league with standings, batting and pitching averages, an official newsletter and even feuds among players. Little Al Jackson used to throw at Tom Tresh all the time. We had a postgame interview show in the garage—*Crystal's Corner*. On Oldtimers' Day we played a two-inning game as old people. We marked our foul lines with fertilizer. It stunk, and we loved it.

I really wanted to be a professional baseball player, but I had a problem. I know it's hard to believe, but I was short as a child. Very short. My brothers were both taller. Much taller.

Don't get me started.

The saddest words I ever heard were, "Maybe five-foot-nine." That's what the doctor said when my mother took me in to be examined for shortness two months before my bar mitzvah. "Maybe five-foot-nine."

Mom was afraid she had a midget wrestler on her hands. The doctor gave me appetite pills. I gained thirty pounds in two months, but I didn't grow an inch. At my bar mitzvah, I stood on a soda box two feet high. I was bursting out of my bar mitzvah suit.

I hate when that happens.

I played baseball anyway. I was shortstop and captain of the high school team. Tony Kornheiser, who's a sports columnist for the Washington *Post,* grew up in Long Beach around the same time I did, and Tony tells people I was a good player. For my size. He says I could've made Triple-A if I'd only been taller. I coulda been a contender.

I went to Marshall University in Huntington, West Virginia, to play second base. I had never been away from home before, not even to camp. The night I arrived, I went to a diner, and the man behind the counter pointed to a sign saying, WE RESERVE THE RIGHT TO REFUSE SERVICE TO ANYONE, then pointed to the mezuzah on my chest and said, "I won't serve you." Welcome to the USA.

Then I found out Marshall had eliminated its baseball program. Not because I was Jewish. They had no money. They also had no dorms. I lived in a hotel for a year. My roommate was twenty-six years old and rebelling against an Amish upbringing. It was a weird year.

I had a radio show on the campus station. It was a call-in show. I used to call in to myself. I'd put my questions on tape and then I'd do the answers live. I'd ask questions like: Should there be an IQ test for basketball players?

When I went home for the summer, I met Janice. We had our first date on July 30, 1966. We went to see the New York Mets play at Shea Stadium and celebrate Casey Stengel's seventy-

Singing "Something Sort of Grandish" from Finian's Rainbow *in 1968. All of these children are married now.*

sixth birthday. He rode in from center field in a chariot.

He looked mahvelous.

So did Janice. She was about to start Nassau Community College. I had never had a date in West Virginia. I transferred to Nassau Community College. We've now been married sixteen years.

With the ultimate cat—Jesse.

THREE

The Most Perceptive Reviews I've Ever Gotten

You can teach me *how to do me.*
> —Muhammad Ali

You talk jazz.
> —Chuck Mangione

How apropos of my life that a young good-looking Jewish man should portray me.
> —Grace Jones

I like you. You're not like the other pig comics.

—Charles Bronson

You are a chameleon.

—Yul Brynner

Who played Sammy in that sketch? Eddie Murphy?

—My mother

You give good Negro.

—Oprah Winfrey

I watched your fucking show last night, and you were fucking great. You did five fucking people in forty fucking minutes, and you were just fucking great.

—Robert De Niro

FOUR

≈≈≈≈≈≈

How I Won the Lottery— and Became a Comedian

Joe Franklin gave me my first big break.

Which he probably doesn't know, because we've never met. But I used to watch his show on WOR-TV all the time when I faked being sick to stay home from school, and I was watching his show again in 1969 when I found out I could stay home from Vietnam without faking being sick.

Joe had his usual lineup of guests: a woman who had slept with W. C. Fields, a man who juggled Siamese fighting fish, and Eddie Can-

"Joe Franklin, my friends, brought to you by Matzos by Streits for the unleavened experience of a lifetime." With Jackie Rodgers, Jr. (Martin Short), Fireman Dan Hallerhan (George Carlin) and Señor Cosa (Christopher Guest).

tor's ghost. "Eddie, my friend, it's very kind of you to materialize for our show," Joe said. "Would you mind telling us what you've been doing lately? Do you see Al Jolson at all?"

I wasn't concentrating on the ghost, the fish or the woman. I was watching the numbers and dates that were flashing across the bottom of the screen, the first hundred birthdays in the first draft lottery that determined which little boys went to fight in Southeast Asia and which little boys stayed home.

I had already seen a list of the second hundred birthdays, and I wasn't in that group. I knew that if I wasn't among the first hundred, I was safe, I didn't have to go play domino theory. It was the best *Joe Franklin Show* I ever saw. My birthday didn't materialize until number 354.

I immediately picked up the telephone and called Dave Hawthorne and Al Finelli, two funny guys I'd met at Nassau Community College, and I said, "I'm out of the lottery, let's go to work." I had transferred to New York University by then, and two nights later Dave and Al came into the city and we started writing sketches. We were an improvisational troupe. Mostly we improvised names. At first we called ourselves We the People. Then we switched to

Boy .. I'm DEPRESSED. .

LIFE IS A
Tough job...

AND THE
HOURS ARE A
BITCH.

by Billy Crystal

the Comedy Jam. Then we became 3's Company. We had more names than we had routines.

We were one of the most popular groups in Eastern college cafeterias. Small Eastern colleges. We weren't ready for the Ivy League. We worked for $150 a week. Split three ways. Before expenses. We traveled in my blue Volkswagen for four-and-a-half years. I still have the Volkswagen sitting in my backyard. It's a reminder.

It reminds me of the time we were at Clarion State College in Pennsylvania. We were working the cafeteria, of course. We had been booked because they thought we were a singing group. We did our act over the sounds of the sizzling hamburgers and the cash register, then started the all-night drive home to Long Island. For once we were using Al's black Volkswagen

With Al and Dave in 3's Company.

instead of my blue one. Al's was the one with the broken windshield wipers.

We drove straight into a blinding snowstorm on the Pennsylvania Turnpike. Once we slid off the road, spun, skidded and managed to get back on the highway. We were grateful until we realized we were heading the wrong way, into traffic. We turned around and decided to follow a truck. The truck turned out to be a sand truck, and it dumped sand all over the Volkswagen, and we lurched off the road again.

The three of us had been gulping No Doz, pure caffeine, to stay awake. We all had cramps, and we couldn't find the edge of the highway, much less a john. We were also freezing. The Long Island seaside air had eaten away the corners of the doors on the Volkswagen, and snow kept blowing in. We barely made it home, cold and cramped. I almost considered getting out of show business.

After all, I had a wife and a baby, and I was making about $4,000 a year, all of it from substitute teaching. I was doing improv as a tax write-off. I actually got audited, and the guy from the IRS saw that I was losing money on the act for years and said, "Why are you in this business?"

"It's in his blood," Janice said.

Then one day I got a phone call from a friend at NYU asking me if I knew a stand-up comedian who could do twenty minutes at a fraternity party for twenty-five dollars. "Sure," I said. "Me."

"How long you been doing stand-up?" he said.

"A long time," I lied.

I didn't have enough material to do five minutes, and I had only four days to put an act together. I need deadlines. I started writing and trying out the material at home. Janice sat on the couch, our only piece of furniture, and Jennifer sat in her high chair, and I performed. I was not overconfident.

"The baby's not laughing," I told Janice.

"She's eighteen months old," Janice said. "What do you want from her?"

I stitched together an act built around Cosell and Ali. Then I walked up four flights of stairs to a roomful of college kids sitting Indian-style, smoking pot. Buddy Morra showed up to watch, and so did Larry Brezner, the junior partners in Rollins, Joffe, Morra & Brezner, the kingmakers of comedy, the group's managers then, my managers now. (The firm represents, among others, Woody Allen, David Letterman and Robin Williams.) They had been after me to try stand-up. I was supposed to do twenty minutes, and I did more than an hour. I exploded. I went nuts and the kids went crazy, and I was back in the living room with the dimes on my head. Buddy and Larry said, "Let's go to work." I felt great, and terrible. I hadn't told Dave and Al that I was going to work alone. I felt like I was cheating on my wife.

The group was booked into The Bitter End in Greenwich Village. We were the opening act for Melissa Manchester. We had finally risen to the middle. I sat down with Dave and Al, my friends and partners for more than four years, and I said, "Guys, if nothing happens this week for us, if nobody discovers us, then I'm going to leave, I'm going to go on my own."

I was praying for nothing to happen because I wanted to go on my own, and we got to the last night of the week. We were down to the last sketch, a Joe Franklin routine, "Memory Lane." I was Joe Franklin, and Al and Dave were playing an old Jewish vaudeville team called Baggy and Pants.

The climax of the piece was supposed to be when Al had a heart seizure in the middle of a joke. Then I would pound him and he'd revive and he'd finish the joke. I pounded him all right. I kicked him all over the stage. "You never took your car," I screamed. "You never paid the tolls." He ended up under Melissa's piano.

But Al topped me. He got up and looked at me and said, "You broke my pen, you *bastard*!"

That was it. The next night I told Al and Dave what I'd done at NYU, that I wanted to do stand-up, and 3's Company parted company. We made our final name change. We changed to nothing.

Obviously, Joe Franklin has played a very big part in my career.

FIVE

≋

The Least Perceptive Reviews I've Ever Gotten

For Rabbit Test, in Which I Played the First Pregnant Man

An abortion.

—Los Angeles *Times*

A miscarriage.

—Chicago *Tribune*

Stillborn.

—Miami *Herald*

As the sinister emcee in Cabaret. *Kenley Summer Stock, 1982.*

Crystal is a humorless unknown who should stay that way.

—Rex Reed
New York *Daily News*

For **Soap**, in Which I Played the First Network Sitcom Homosexual

Mildly frightening:
Hey, fairy, want to do my hair?

Very frightening:
Hi! I play defensive tackle in the National Football League, and I think you're very attractive.

For **Saturday Night Live**, *After the First Show of the 1984–85 Season*

There's a groveling Las Vegassy side to Crystal.

—Tom Shales
Washington *Post*

For Overtipping a Bellhop in Las Vegas and Possibly Groveling

Hey, you don't have to give me anything. I love your stuff. My wife and I saw Cabaret *ten times, Mr. Grey.*

Fernando with Sting—two stars in search of last names.

As Cosell's wife, with Howard nibbling on my neck—right there! P.S. This is not why he left Monday Night Football.

SIX

I Opened for Neil Sedaka— and Closed for Chemotherapy

I was a pig in a blanket, an opening act, an hors d'oeuvre. I was supposed to whet appetites, which meant I had about the same chance of survival as a shrimp on a toothpick.

I opened for Sha Na Na in Baltimore one night in the mid-seventies. They were big. They were so big, I didn't get billing. No one told the audience there was an opening act.

I drove from Long Island to Baltimore, four-and-a-half hours in my Volkswagen, thinking about what I was going to do, and when I got there I found out the theater was in the round. I had never worked a theater in the round. I didn't know what to do. Do I make the same face in four different directions? Do I keep spinning while I'm talking? Could I have more anxiety?

The theater made me uneasy. So did the audience. Half the people were dressed like Sha Na Na. Nobody was dressed like me. I wore a velvet jacket and a bow tie. At eight the lights went down, and the audience started cheering. Then a disembodied voice said, "Ladies and gentlemen, no smoking in the theater," and the cheering stopped. "No drinking in the theater." They booed. "No picture taking." Eichmann got a warmer reception in Jerusalem.

Then they heard: "Now, to *start* our show"— followed by salt for the wound—"please welcome a funny young comedian from New York." Hostility filled the room. I got a contact low. Bring in a lion, I figured, and let him eat me, and then they'll be happy.

I took a huge bow in four directions and said, "Thank you, thank you, I've always called Baltimore home."

Half the people laughed. The other half kept yelling, "Get off the fucking stage." I managed to turn them around, too. I hit them with all my good material, all twenty minutes' worth. I started with Ali and Cosell and finished with *The Exorcist,* shining a flashlight in my own face, exorcising the demon, who turned out to be Richard Nixon possessed by his tapes. I got a standing ovation and a check for $125, and climbed in the Volkswagen and drove four-and-a-half hours so that I could sleep in my own bed.

Over and over, all the way home, I listened to a tape of the show. I listened to the lines, and the laughter.

I miss those days, those midnight hours on the turnpike with nothing on the road but trucks and me, and nothing on my mind but the act and how I could make it funnier.

.   .   .

I got billing when I opened for Neil Sedaka in Tonawanda, New York. I got billing till a reviewer said the show featured a rising young star and a fading rocker. That night my name came off the marquee. My daughter Jennifer, who was then three, didn't bring Neil and me any closer when she playfully told him, "You sound like a girl."

"How would you like your head shaved?" said Sedaka.

Jenny got more diplomatic as she got older. Once, when she was about four, she was in a store with Janice, and she said, "Look, Mommy, a black lady. Black. Black."

Stung, the woman turned and glared, and Jenny sensed her pain.

"Which is my favorite color," Jenny said.

• • •

When Janice traveled with me, when Jenny was young, we had a very romantic life on the road. I would bring home food after the last show, and while Jenny slept in our motel room, Janice and I would sit in privacy, if not comfort, on the floor of the bathroom, spread a towel over the toilet seat and turn it into our dinner table. I told people we dined in marble halls.

• • •

I enjoyed my tour of the Midwest with Melissa Manchester. She always sold out, which meant I had no pressure on me. If I did well, I was a bonus, a surprise. I experimented. I learned. I'd open each night, watch Melissa, run to the bus, strap myself in, watch videotapes till I fell asleep, then be awakened around 4:00 A.M. when we reached the next stop. Then we'd check into a motel and go back to sleep. I had only one bad moment, in Ohio, when a guy came backstage and said, "Are you the comedian?"

I confessed.

"Do you do any Jew or nigger jokes?" he said.

"Only about thirty minutes," I said. "Why?"

"Well," he said, "we have forty junior members of the Ku Klux Klan coming to the show tonight."

They were a great audience. They didn't lynch me. I did all Bob Newhart material.

· · ·

The first night I opened for Billy Joel, I had never met him. I did twenty minutes, and when he came on stage, the first thing he said was, "I ain't saying a word."

It was a lovely compliment.

I reciprocated. I didn't sing, and I didn't marry Christie Brinkley.

· · ·

Sometimes I had trouble opening a show to an audience that had timed its drugs for the head-liner. Once, when I was reenacting a Rhonda Fleming–Victor Mature jungle film, I asked for a volunteer to help with the sound effects, to bury her hands in a bowl of potato chips and crunch the chips to match my stealthy steps through the brush. A woman offered her services, and just as she bent over the bowl, her Quaaludes kicked in, and her head sank into the chips. It was terrible. She missed half my act.

In Lake Tahoe I solicited a volunteer for the same number, and the most beautiful blonde I had ever seen, with the biggest bosoms spilling out of the lowest-cut dress, raced up from the back of the room and bounced onto the stage. I took one look at them, at her, and fell over backward. "This is a Jewish nightmare," I said. "You meet the *shiksa* goddess of your dreams, and there's a thousand people watching."

I said, "Hello," and asked her what she did. She said, "Everything. I love oysters of all kinds."

I explained to her how to do the sound effects, and the first step I took, she leaned over and squashed the potato chips with her tits. "I should have brought dip," I said.

The routine usually lasted six to eight minutes. I stretched it to forty. After the show, I asked the maitre d' where her table was. I wanted to send champagne to her, and her two friends. The maitre d' told me not to bother. The blonde, he explained, was being well paid to help a governor of one of the fifty states get over the dismaying fact that his wife had not made the trip to Nevada with him.

. . .

Eventually, of course, I became a closing act. I closed a medical convention in Miami. I came on right after a film called *Chemotherapy Then, Chemotherapy Now*. The film showed patients in varying degrees of agony. "Notice how the loss of hair has been minimized." The audience applauded when the film terminated. "And now we have some entertainment. I personally have never seen him, but I hear he's pretty good."

For my opening number, I did a radical mastectomy.

. . .

I wouldn't say it was easier to follow cancer than Uncle Heavy and His Singing Pigs, but it was close. Uncle Heavy weighed about five hundred pounds. He traveled with his wife, who was four-foot-six, and with his pigs, who dressed like me. They wore bow ties and sunglasses. They skipped the velvet jacket. Uncle Heavy wore overalls. Designer overalls. The Babar label.

We appeared together at Davidson College in North Carolina. I'm glad we didn't tour. The pigs didn't really sing. They squealed. Uncle Heavy would sing, "How dry I . . . ," and then he'd pinch a pig, and the pig would go, "Arrrggghhh," and then Uncle Heavy would go, "How wet I'll . . . ," and pinch another pig.

I watched from the wings. I couldn't believe it. "Who booked this?" I said. The pigs were shitting all over the stage, and I had to go out and follow them.

It was great to be a headliner at last.

"Don't get me started."—*Buddy Young, Jr.*

SEVEN

Baiting the Hook—I Love When I Do That

Jazz musicians, the first gods of my childhood, start with a theme, and then go off and improvise, and then come back to the theme, and when they stop blowing, you remember the theme long after you've forgotten the great solos.

That's the *hook*—the sound you keep hearing after the music stops.

You have to have a hook in comedy, too. You have to have something to remember after the comic walks offstage.

I try to sink hooks into all my characters. I try to give each one his own look, his own voice. I try to give each one a special phrase, his trademark.

When I say, "I hate when I do that," or, "I hate when that happens," my audience knows that Willie, the masochist, has probably just put his tongue in a self-threading movie projector—just to see how far in he could get it to go.

When I say, "Unbelieeevuble," or, "Amazing," my audience knows that Ricky, the bowler, is likely to follow up with one of his backward insults: "Could he have more hair in his ears? Could he brush his teeth less often?"

When I say, "Don't get me started," or "What we need is love today," my audience knows that Buddy Young, Jr., the cigar-smoking comic, is about to expose his ego or his bitterness.

Sammy says, "And I mean that."

Joe Franklin says, "My friends."

The old black musician says, "Can you dig that? I knew that you could."

But the ultimate hook is Fernando's.

I kept count one day, and 170 people walked up to me and said, "You look mahvelous."

Senator Kennedy and Mayor Koch have both told me that I look marvelous, and so have Sting and Julian Lennon, Dick Van Dyke and Jesse Jackson. Jackson told me I looked marvelous as a black, which is as close as you can get to an official endorsement. Stevie Wonder told me I *sounded* marvelous. When Pete Rose got his big hit, MAHVELOUS was flashed on the scoreboard. When the astronauts were orbiting the Earth, and Houston asked how the Earth looked, the reply came back: "Mahvelous." Tom Heinsohn said it during a game, Johnny Carson almost said it, and the delivery boy from the drugstore won't stop saying it.

And once, at a basketball game at Madison Square Garden, as Bernard King of the Knicks stepped to the foul line, Mo Cheeks of the Philadelphia 76ers spotted me at courtside and shouted, "It's Mr. Mahvelous! Yo, Bernard! It's the mahvelous man!"

The hook has been a hit since the first time I used it, and now it is so deeply planted, I no longer have to say it. I can say, "You look . . ." or sometimes only, "You . . ." and, automatically, the audience finishes the phrase. It's been going on for two years, and I can't explain why. All I know is . . .

It's unbelieeevuble! It's amazing!

And I mean that.

With Mr. T and Hulk Hogan. "So tell me dahlings, what are your plans for Passover?"

EIGHT

Hitting Bottom— Saturday Night Dead

It was opening night, the first *Saturday Night Live* ever. It was Chevy and John and Gilda and Dan, and George Carlin was the host, and I was a special guest. October 11, 1975, I still have the script, a collector's item. Right at the end, it says, "George Carlin—Introduction," and then, "Billy Crystal—Monologue to Come." It never came.

I was supposed to do the jungle movie. Don Pardo, the announcer, was going to crunch the potato chips. He was safe. He didn't use

Quaaludes, and his tits were mediocre. I was going to play Rhonda Fleming and Victor Mature and the tarantula that was threatening to come between them.

I knew I was about to become a star. Lorne Michaels, the producer, told me I was going to appear on the show six times its first year, and the sixth time I would probably host the show. I was in ecstasy. Then Lorne told me I would be going on at 12:55 A.M., the final slot on the first show. I was in agony. I feared that the last thing in the lineup would be the first thing to go.

On Friday night we did a dress rehearsal for the NBC executives. They loved the potato chips. Lorne Michaels didn't like the length. I ran six minutes and eleven seconds.

"What do you want?" I said.

"Two minutes," he said.

"You want me to cut out two minutes?" I said.

"I want you to leave in two minutes," he said.

I was devastated. The tarantula couldn't crawl across Rhonda Fleming's chest in two minutes, and I didn't have anyone else I could do in such a short time. I crawled home to Long Beach shaken.

On Saturday Buddy Morra, my manager, argued with Lorne. He pleaded. We lost. Lorne Michaels had more pressing problems. The show was very long. Carlin was very angry. NBC wanted him to wear a suit. He wanted to wear a T-shirt. They compromised. He wore a T-shirt and a suit.

I was out. I was cut. I reacted like a man. I cried.

I walked out of the studio on the eighth floor of NBC less than two hours before the first show went on the air. Tears streaked my makeup. Gilda chased after me. (It would have sounded better if Chevy had chased.) "What happened?" she said.

"I don't know," I said. "It's not working out."

In a daze, I took a cab to Penn Station and then an hour train ride to Long Beach. At least I knew I wouldn't starve. I was carrying a suitcase full of potato chips.

I sat on the train with my head bouncing off the grimy window like Dustin Hoffman at the end of *Midnight Cowboy*. The worst was still to come. I had to call the relatives, tell them they didn't have to stay up till one in the morning.

Janice was waiting. "What happened?" she said.

"I got bumped," I said. "The show was too long."

We turned on NBC, and from the moment Chevy said, "Live from New York, it's . . . ," I knew the show was going to be great. I knew that despite all its problems it was going to work, and I knew that I should have been part of it. I belonged there.

I didn't do six shows the first year of *SNL*. I did one, finally, in April 1976. By then *Saturday Night Live* was a huge hit, and the show I was on drew an enormous audience. I'd like to take the credit, but the fact that Ron Nessen, the presidential press secretary, was the host, and his boss, President Ford, opened the show by announcing, "Live from New York . . . ," probably had something to do with it. I did "Face," my monologue of an old black jazz musician. I got good reviews, great reaction. I wasn't on the show again for the next eight years.

I was hurt. I've experienced other professional disasters—the sudden death of *The Billy Crystal Comedy Hour,* the unfortunate life of the film *Rabbit Test*—but nothing cut quite so deeply as the loss of the original *Saturday Night Live*.

"It was wrong, man," Belushi told me years later when I bumped into him. "It was fucking wrong. They fucked you, man."

John had become a big star. So had Chevy and Gilda and Dan. I was doing fine. I was in Hollywood, doing *Soap*. But I knew that wasn't where I was supposed to be. I was three thousand miles away from where I should have been.

I went home on March 17, 1984. I celebrated St. Patrick's Day by hosting *Saturday Night Live*.

As Kate and Ali (with the great Martin Short).

Lou Goldman: "The forecast for Thursday: Don't be such a big shot. Take a jacket."

NINE

Titles I Thought Would Help Sell This Book

Iacocca II

Elvis and Priscilla and Me

I Always *Played the Game*

Wise Ass

The Bibble

Crystal's Honor

The Color Crystal

Muammar Dearest

TEN

I Want to Be Me—or an Old Jewish Man or a Sexy Black Lady

I don't want to brag, but I think I could play an old black Jew in drag better than Olivier. I'm comfortable being old. I'm comfortable being black. I'm comfortable being Jewish. And I look very good in dresses.

I like twisting my face and my voice and my mind into different characters. I feel at home in other bodies.

But I do have a specialty. When I'm in trouble, under pressure, I fall back on being old and

Jewish. I rattle phlegm. I break wind. I feel good.

I've known people who were old and Jewish all my life. When I was a baby, my grandmother moved to Long Beach to die, which she did, twenty-eight years later. For twenty-eight years I watched her play a terrific funny old Jewish person.

One night, when Janice and I were teenagers and dating, we shared a bedroom with my grandmother. (If you're looking for titillation, stop here, forget it.) We had three separate beds, and my grandmother slept in the middle bed because, in the first place, Janice and I weren't allowed to sleep together, and in the second, I didn't know how. Right after we got in bed with the lights out, my grandmother farted. It was a tense moment. Janice and I struggled not to laugh. My grandmother broke the tension. "What do you want?" she said. "I didn't eat roses."

My grandmother is in my act. So are most of my relatives. Pieces of them. Shifted around. I have to be careful with names. I can't use real names. They're touchy. They're also litigious. Except Julius. I can use Julius. Both of my grandfathers were named Julius. Each one would think it was the other.

I have the same problem with my two best-known characters: Fernando and Sammy. I can't use their real names, either. I kid you. I'm a kidder. I love them, those fellows, Fernando and Sammy, Lamas & Davis, a law firm specializing in immigration cases.

I thought Fernando Lamas was one of the great guests in the history of *The Tonight Show,* one of the few who could actually manipulate Johnny. Fernando could tug at the crease of his trousers so suavely he made everyone else look slovenly. He looked . . . good. He was bright and funny, and his accent was no accident, his sophistication no sham. He knew who he was.

I started doing Fernando over the telephone. I create a lot of my characters on the phone. I first did Fernando on the phone to David Steinberg, another of my gurus at Rollins, Joffe, Morra & Brezner. David is not the comedian David Steinberg, but he is a very comic David Steinberg. He loved my Fernando. "And how is Esther?" he asked.

"She looks mahvelous," I told him.

I never met the real Fernando. He was still alive when I started doing him in my act, but he died before "You look . . ." became a craze. I met his widow, Esther Williams, in 1985 at The Night of 100 Stars. Morgan Fairchild, who was

"They look mahvelous."

my first guest ever in the Hideaway, said I had to meet Esther. I said I had to get out of my Fernando makeup before I met Esther. I finally got up enough courage to introduce myself. She still looked marvelous. Esther told me that the real Fernando loved my Fernando.

My Fernando is a caricature, a distorted reflection. He interviews the Korean comic, Johnny Yune, calls him "Johnny U" and asks him about his days with the Baltimore Colts. He interviews Cathy Lee Crosby and asks her why she sold Bing's things. He interviews Siskel and Ebert and asks them which is which. The real Fernando always knew what was what.

My Sammy, I think, strikes closer to home. I opened for Sammy twenty-eight times in fourteen days, and I watched him perform twenty-eight times in fourteen days. It was like going to school, watching a master. I would come to the theater two hours early to sit with Sammy and listen to his stories. He knew everybody. He knew Bogart. He knew Tracy. I think he knew eleven of the twelve apostles, and he missed the last sit-down only because he had another gig.

I studied Sammy's jewelry, his boots, the way he spoke, the way he smoked, the way he moved. Still, even I wasn't prepared for the way I looked when Peter Montagna, the makeup man at *Saturday Night Live,* first transformed me into Sammy. I cracked up. The resemblance was uncanny. I couldn't blame my mother for not recognizing me. She didn't believe it was me till I told her over the phone, "Mom, you're my main lady, and I mean that."

The real Sammy said my Sammy was a gas, but out of date. "You do the *old* me," said the new Sammy, "and I mean that."

Peter Montagna also did the makeup for my video. He is a genius. He can make me look like Manute Bol after God made me look like Spud Webb.

Peter put me through hours of torture, punishing my skin to promote my career. He made me into Prince and Grace Jones and Tina Turner. I knew I'd be a good Prince. I have some Moroccan blood. I knew I'd be a good Grace Jones. We have similar cheekbones. And I knew I'd be a good Tina Turner. We have similar legs. In fact, after Peter turned me into Tina, a stagehand told me, "You have great legs." I said, "Thank you," in as deep a voice as I could.

I enjoy impersonations—I have more fun being Cosell than he does and I could play Joe Franklin forever, as he has—but I enjoy creat-

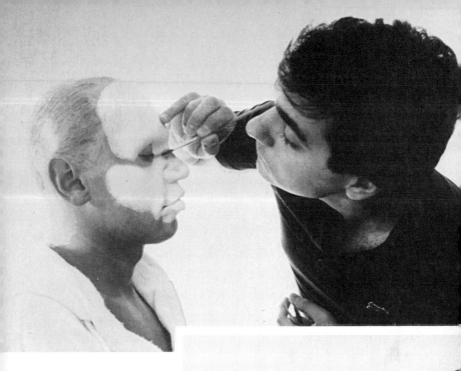

It's not Mr. Potato Head

. . . it's not Manute Bol

. . . it's Grace Jones!

76

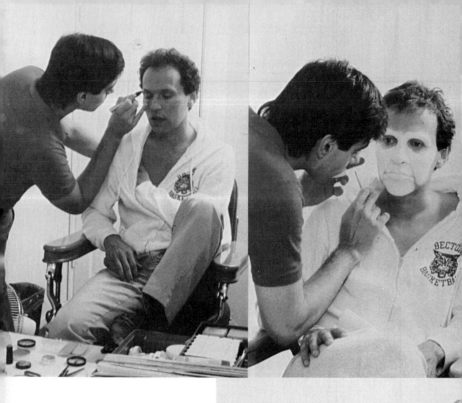

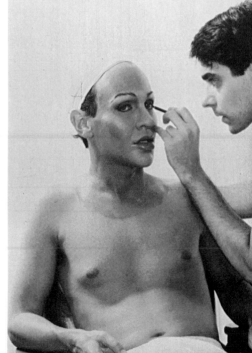

Starting from scratch . . . instant Private Dancer.

78

ing my own characters even more, shaping them, bringing them to life, giving each face and voice his own personality.

The old black musician who delivers the monologue to "Face" is, obviously, a survivor of my childhood. But he is more. He is a symbol of my father, who died when I was only fifteen, and when the musician says, "Can you dig that? I knew that you could," I am talking, through him, to my father, seeking and gaining his approval for my career. I want him to know that the gorilla masks worked.

Leonard "the Rooster" Willoughby is the ballplayer I always wanted to be, lightning-fast, skilled, easygoing yet dignified. As a player, he moved without wasted energy; as an old man, he still does.

Penny Lane is a transvestite, a woman trapped in a man's body, playing wistful songs in a piano bar, cynical yet vulnerable. She has dreams. And nightmares.

Buddy Young, Jr., is a hundred comics I've known, loud, confident, cloying, sometimes even funny, a man who lives life on the brink of being obnoxious.

Willie started off as an autograph hound, a mild form of dementia—*You anybody? Who's in town, Mr. Crystal? Who's here? Can you just sign these twelve pictures for me?*—but he blossomed the night Chris Guest and I sat down and, facing a void and a deadline, desperately improvised the first masochistic dialogue between Willie and Frankie. Chris is brilliant— the greatest improviser I've ever worked with. Willie is Dopey, who was always my favorite dwarf. Willie's got a big smile. He's just happy to be there. He's a lot like me.

Ricky is the guys I grew up with, the guys I played ball with, unpolished, unsophisticated, a survivor of Vietnam and mescaline and terminal horniness and yet, somehow, sweet. He's like everybody. He wants to be a director. Marcos, too. Duvalier. Qaddafi. They all want to be directors. Ricky is nicer than they are. He even feels sorry for Qaddafi. He thinks his problem is his name. Muammar. The kids all made fun of him. *Oh, Muammar. Come here, Muammar.* He has to hate his parents for naming him Muammar, and he sees Reagan as the ultimate parent, the oldest of the old, and so he takes out his anger on Reagan. *Ray-gun.* That's what Ricky calls him.

When I was asked to do a piece for the Jerry Lewis telethon, for the Muscular Dystrophy Association, I thought of Ricky right away, and I thought of Danny Sullivan, who was from Long

"Unbelieeevuble."
—*Ricky*

Beach and was a very good athlete, in a wheel-chair. I always used to pick Danny on my soft-ball team. He'd bat, and I'd be his designated runner. The telethon made me think of Danny, and then, as I rode around in my car, which is where I do my best writing, I came up with an idea for Ricky.

In high school, I decided, Ricky knew a girl named Ellen Fortunato, who was in a wheel-chair. Ricky found out she'd never been to the beach, so he took her. He carried her down to the water.

I was real careful with her, you know, like with the groceries, you know, when you got eggs in the bag.

Gently, tenderly, Ricky laid Ellen down by the water's edge and let the waves lap up against her feet.

Like she giggled, you know, 'cause she liked it. It was four o'clock when the beach is at its best. I mean, I don't like to go early because everyone's fat and oiled up, and it's crowded and hairy, but at four o'clock, the beach is mine. And she really liked it. You could tell. She had this smile on her face that was like beautiful.

Twenty years later, Ricky went to his high school reunion.

It was unbelieeevuble. I mean, I kept saying to people, "Could you like have more bellies? Is that possible? Hey, Ira, could you like be more of a dentist?" And then I started looking for her. I wanted to see her. But all I could find was a picture of her, and it said, "Rest in Peace, Class of '65." And I felt bad. But then I thought about it. And I felt okay. Because I saw that smile, and I remembered it, and I knew I was the only one who ever saw that four o'clock smile. It was unbelieeevuble.

ELEVEN

I Just Called to Say Hello

"Hi, Aunt Sophie. It's Billy. I just called to say hello."

"Oh, my God, it's you, I'm *plotzing*. We're so proud of you, darling. The whole card group, they want pictures. I said I wouldn't bother you. It's no bother? That's very sweet of you. Just a few. Thirty-seven pictures. Do you have a pencil for the names? I don't want to bother you, darling, I'll send you the list."

"Would you give me the phone? Billy, it's your uncle. How's Merv? Do you still see Merv? When are you doing Merv? You're not doing Merv? You're doing Letterman? Oh, that's too late. Your aunt says that's too late. And between you and I, he's not my cup of tea. I like Merv. The other night, he had on all these co-

ALFRED...

I Forgot to call my
MOTHER LAST WEEK...

by Billy Crystal

ShE Took it
WEU...

ShE put my
piCTuRE oN A
MIIK CARToN.

medians. Jan Murray. Shecky Greene. Nipsey. Russell. You know another Nipsey? It was a very nice show. It had a theme. Comedians. But I was surprised none of them mentioned you. Are they mad at you?"

"No, they're not mad at him. Listen, darling, it's your aunt again. I'm fine. I'm retaining too much water. Otherwise I'm fine. How's the weather out there? You're here? You're at the Pierre? Very fancy. Why don't you come by and we'll order Chinks? We'll put some dimes on your head. You have plans, darling? I understand. I'm not hurt. It's your life. We're just family. Anyway . . ."

"Billy, it's your uncle again. I've got ankle bracelets for the kids. E.T. ankle bracelets. Don't worry, I've got plenty. For some reason, they didn't move. They're white gold. They'll love them. They have a standard clasp. Tell me, have you seen Elizabeth Taylor? She's a convert, you know. We'll take it. Yeah. She became a Jew for Eddie Fisher. Or Mike Todd. Or Richard Burton. She did it for somebody. Or everybody. I don't know. Do you see Eddie at all?"

"Would you give me the—?"

"When you start paying the bills here."

"It's your aunt again, darling. We'll try to stay up. He's not Jewish, is he, Letterman? But some of the guests are? Good. I'll watch for you and then I'll turn it off. He leaves me cold. I know you like him. You love him. Do you get residuals for that?"

"It's your uncle. Have a good trip. Don't be such a stranger. Say hi to Elizabeth Taylor if you see her. And Merv."

"Goodbye, darling, I just want to tell you one thing: You sound mahvelous! I had to say it. I'm *plotzing*. Goodbye, darling."

[Click.]

"Why do you have to start with Merv Griffin . . . ?"

TWELVE

Close and Casual Encounters with the Great and Near-Great

Even the elevator was dropping names, in the most bizarre combinations: Lucille Ball, Eddie Arcaro and Laurence Olivier on one floor, Martha Graham, Joe DiMaggio and Rock Hudson on another. They popped up everywhere at Radio City Music Hall, these stars of The Night of 100 Stars, and I couldn't help it, my eyes kept widening, my jaw dropping. One of the sweeter fringe benefits of my work is that I often get to see people close up I once thought were ten feet tall on movie screens—or ten inches tall on TV.

Most of them turn out to be somewhere in between.

. . .

I was going to NYU and working as an usher at a theater playing *You're a Good Man, Charlie Brown* when Walter Cronkite handed me his ticket stub. I led him by flashlight to his seat, then knelt down, shined the flashlight in my own face and said, "Mr. Cronkite, if there's anything I can do to help you in any way during the show, please don't hesitate to let me know." Then, automatically, without thinking, I flipped the flashlight into his face as though it were a hand mike. "Yes, there is," Walter Cronkite said. "You can take the flashlight out of my eyes."

. . .

On a hot August day in the early 1970s, as I stood at the corner of Fifty-seventh Street and Seventh Avenue, the WALK sign blinked on, and a hand touched my back. I was frightened till I heard the voice. "Excuse me," he said. "Could you help me get across the street? I don't see so well anymore." I had imitated the voice so many times. It was an honor to help Jackie Robinson cross the street.

•   •   •

I was in Las Vegas for the first time, participating in a Dean Martin roast for Muhammad Ali, and backstage after the show I saw Orson Welles sitting uncomfortably on a little stool. I loved him. When I was studying film at NYU, Martin Scorcese, who was my teacher, showed us *Citizen Kane* twice a week. I was awed. I walked up to him and said, "Excuse me, Mr. Welles. My name is Billy Crys—"

"I know."

"—and I just want to say—"

Welles finished my sentence: "—that I was a big influence on you and that you really loved what I did in the films and that's really great and thank you very much and goodbye."

I was dismissed, and dismayed. I walked away shaking, I was so wounded.

•   •   •

When I moved to California in the mid-1970s, Rob Reiner and I became best friends. He took me to a charity tennis tournament, and I found myself playing doubles against Rob's father Carl and Mel Brooks. This isn't fair, I thought. These guys made me want to be a comedian. I know all their pieces. I wore out their record. Mel yelled at me, "You. You. Wake up. The Jew is serving. Are you a Jew? Yes? I'll take it easy on you. The Jew is serving."

I couldn't hit the ball.

Several years later, after Max Brooks and Jennifer Crystal became third-grade class-mates, Mel and I reported to the same PTA meeting. *People* magazine would have loved to cover the meeting. Besides Mel and his wife, Anne Bancroft, Eileen Brennan, the actress, was there, and so was Michael Eisner, who ran Paramount Pictures. We were all crunched into third-grade chairs with our knees tucked under third-grade desks.

The teacher told us that to celebrate National Book Week, each child who purchased five books through the school would receive an overseas pen pal.

Mel couldn't resist. He raised his hand and waved it as though he needed to leave the room, quickly. I started to giggle.

"Mr. Brooks?" the teacher said.

"Present," Mel said.

"But seriously," he added. "Does the child

have to *buy* the books outright? Can't he just option them and then sell them to Michael Eisner's son, to be developed into junior major motion pictures?"

I broke up.

"Forget about pen pals," Mel said. "We're talking big bucks here."

$$\bullet \quad \bullet \quad \bullet$$

I would love to be Woody Allen (half the time, anyway), writing, directing and acting in films (and Lily Tomlin the other half, performing an intelligent, cohesive, funny, biting act). Woody is one of the people who overwhelms me, dazzles me with his talent. The first time I met him, we played basketball, two-on-two, at a gym he had rented in a church in Manhattan. I was invited by a mutual friend. Woody arrived in a limousine, carrying a Bloomingdale's shopping bag, with a ball inside. We talked jazz. We talked clarinet. I told him Pee Wee Russell taught me how to play. Woody knew my dad from the Central Plaza. "He used to let me in without proof of age," Woody said, "because he knew I liked the music."

At first I guarded Woody. "Not too close," he said. "It makes me nauseous." Then we teamed up, and even though the other two guys were much taller, we clicked, we beat them easily. Woody kept giving me high fives. I was in heaven. I didn't see Woody again until nine years later, after he'd made *Hannah and Her Sisters*. I saw him in Elaine's—my first visit— and I told him how much I loved his film. He told me he loved my Joe Franklin. I was so nervous. I didn't think he'd remember me. "Why would he think I wouldn't remember him?" Woody told our mutual friend afterward. "He had such a good jump shot."

·　·　·

One afternoon on *The Mike Douglas Show* I sat down between a pair of giants, Lucille Ball and Jimmy Stewart. I wanted to impress them. "Mr. Stewart," I said, "I'm a huge fan of yours. I've seen *Gone with the Wind* nine times."

The audience fell apart. Lucy fell off the couch laughing, and Stewart, knowing what I was up to, measured his words as he always does, and said, "Yeah, I did some of my best work in that." So for at least one moment I acted with Jimmy Stewart.

·　·　·

During my *Saturday Night Live* year, I picked up my daughter Lindsay at her school in Manhattan one day and we walked in the rain to the corner of Third Avenue and Sixteenth Street to wait for a cab. Directly in front of us a car stopped for the light, and I recognized the shape of the face of the passenger. It was Katharine Hepburn. Just then she turned, and Lindsay saw her and said, "The *Golden Pond* lady," and Katharine Hepburn looked at her and smiled and gave a little wave and drove away in the rain.

• • •

One time Christopher Guest and I were up at 3:00 A.M. to be made into Rooster Willoughby and King Carl Johnson for *SNL*. We went in as two thirty-six-year-old white men, and came out four-and-a-half hours later as seventy-five-year-old blacks. As we got on the elevator at Rockfeller Center, we ran into Dan Aykroyd, who was there to do the *Today* show.

"Howya doin'?" Chris drawled in his best King Carl voice.

"Good morning, sir," Dan answered.

"I didn't like *Neighbors*," Chris said, leading him on.

"I'm sorry." Dan replied politely.

"We didn't like it at *all*," I continued. "We *hated* it." Dan started looking around for a way out. "'Cause your hair was so weird."

Then he took a closer look at us and caught on. We all laughed hysterically. "It's amazing what makeup can do," Dan said.

• • •

When Ringo Starr hosted *SNL,* I joined him— as Sammy—for a duet. In rehearsal I got up enough nerve to ask him about John Lennon. "When he walked into a room," Ringo said, "it was like everyone else was quiet even if they were talking. He had a presence. I loved him, and I miss him."

• • •

Once, at a small Italian restaurant on the edge of Harlem, I saw Roy Cohn sitting at a table on one side of me, and Claus von Bulow sitting at a table on the other. I knew I hadn't died and gone to heaven. I figured I was the only one in the restaurant without a taster.

• • •

I worshiped Mickey Mantle. The first game I went to at Yankee Stadium, in 1956, I sat in Louis Armstrong's seats, and Mickey signed my scorecard and hit a home run, and from then on, whenever I went to the Stadium, I thought Mickey knew I was there and was telling him-

Dream come true.

self, "Billy's here. I better have a good day. I better try to hit one for him."

More than a quarter of a century later, Mickey and I worked together on a baseball special preceding the All-Star Game, and at the end of the show—I had written the script—we stood on a field in Cooperstown, where the game was invented, and we tossed a ball back and forth. "Nice catch, kid," Mickey said, and then, when I threw a ball wildly beyond his reach, he yelled, "Hey, don't make me run. If I could run, I'd still be playing." And I grinned, with tears in my eyes.

•   •   •

I was playing shortstop in a celebrity game at Dodger Stadium in front of 50,000 people, and on a ground ball up the middle, I raced over, fought off a bad hop, cut off the ball, spun and threw to Kareem Abdul-Jabbar at first base for the out. "Hey, that was a major-league play," said Reggie Smith of the Dodgers. Later, I hit a triple to the opposite field, and after the game one of the Dodger officials asked me how old I was. "Early thirties," I said, and he looked disappointed. "Good game, anyway," he said. I got the feeling that if I had said eighteen, I might have had a shot at Albuquerque next year.

Dodger Stadium, 1985. Ozzie Smith, eat your heart out. Or, last of the great Jewish shortstops.

• • •

It wasn't the first time I had played with Kareem. When he was at Power Memorial Academy in Manhattan, when his name was Lew Alcindor, he had a classmate from Long Beach who was a good friend of mine. Lew would come out to visit and we'd play "Bird" in my backyard. Once the three of us went to the schoolyard and got into a three-on-three winner-stays-on-the-halfcourt game, and with Lew on our side, we stayed on the court all afternoon (and technically twenty years later we still are on the court).

Opening day. A guy can dream, can't he? (At the Houston Astrodome.)

• • •

I never saw Joe DiMaggio play, but my father pointed him out to me at an oldtimers' game and told me he was the greatest. Years later, the night of the Ali-Holmes fight, I went out to dinner in Las Vegas with a group of people, and DiMaggio happened to be in the group. He spoke only once during dinner, to the maître d'. "Too much cheese in the antipasto," Joe D. said. He left the dining room with his strong, special stride, a John Wayne walk, and I heard someone say, "Look, there goes Mr. Coffee."

• • •

When I auditioned, unsuccessfully, for *Death of a Salesman* with Dustin Hoffman, I met Arthur Miller and got him to autograph a copy of the play for me. He told me that he was fascinated by stand-up comedy and that his earliest writing, in fact, had been a pair of humorous monologues for himself. Miller said he learned quickly, however, that he was better at making people cry than laugh.

And all I kept thinking, standing with this brilliant man, was: This guy slept with Marilyn Monroe.

Leonard
"the Rooster"
Willoughby,
circa 1932.

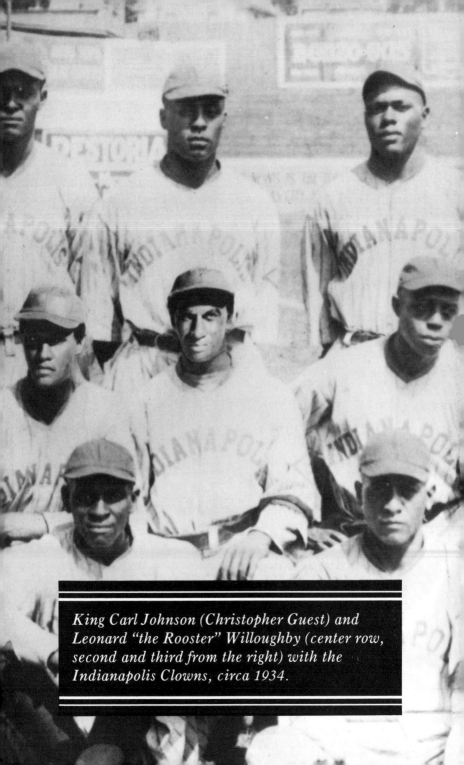

King Carl Johnson (Christopher Guest) and Leonard "the Rooster" Willoughby (center row, second and third from the right) with the Indianapolis Clowns, circa 1934.

Happy in retirement, 1985: "The trouble with baseball is, there ain't no real grass no more."

THIRTEEN

Ricky, Willie, Buddy and Penny —on the Air with Dr. Green

Good evening, ladies and gentlemen, I'm Dr. Stanley Green. We're coming to you on 98 FM here in Waco, Connecticut, and I am a sex therapist. I feel your pain. I know you're out there. We have a toll-free number. Eddie's my engineer, so give me a call. Remember, the first step to becoming well sexually is to admit that you're having trouble. So pick up a phone. Reach out and touch . . . Hello? You're on the air with Dr. Stanley Green.

Ricky: Hello, Dr. Green.

Dr. Green: Yes? What's your name?

Ricky: Like I can't tell you. I'm too embarrassed. It's unbelieeevuble. It's amazing. I'm having trouble with my boner.

Dr. Green: Okay, sir, that's not uncommon. What seems to be the problem?

Ricky: I suffer from premature orgasm.

Dr. Green: How premature?

Ricky: Well, it usually happens in the car, on the way over to pick up the girl. Like could I come any sooner?

Dr. Green: Do you have a radio in your car?

Ricky: Yes.

Dr. Green: Try an all-news station. It might help.

Ricky: I have another problem, Dr. Green.

Dr. Green: Yes.

Ricky: I'm a frequent masturbator.

Dr. Green: So what's the problem? How do you feel when you beat the bishop?

Ricky: Like I feel ashamed.

Dr. Green: Are you married?

Ricky: No.

Dr. Green: So what are you complaining about? At least you have something.

Ricky: But could I feel worse about it?

Dr. Green: You know what you should do. Your whole approach is wrong. Masturbating is not a bad thing. It's a good thing. You don't have to try and get a cab for your hand late at night. But let me make a suggestion: Why don't you put some romance back in the relationship between you and your hand? Treat your hand better. Take your hand out to a nice restaurant and maybe buy the bottle of wine you always wanted but never had the money for. Maybe take a long walk with your hand, by the river. And when you get to your apartment, don't kiss your hand right away. Let there be some mystery. Maybe don't look at your hand for a few days. And don't phone. Don't take your hand for granted. And then, when you're in the mood, when it feels right, turn down the lights, put on a Tony Bennett record and jerk off. Hello? You're on the air with Dr. Stanley Green.

Willie: Dr. Green?

Dr. Green: Yes. What's your name?

Frankie (Christopher Guest) and Willie: They hate *when that happens.*

Willie: My name is Willie.

Dr. Green: What do you do, Willie?

Willie: I'm a messenger slash night watchman.

Dr. Green: Ah, goal-oriented. I like that. What's your problem, Willie?

Willie: Well, I have some, you know, strange sexual habits, I guess.

Dr. Green: What do you mean?

Willie: You know, when I take one of them . . .

Dr. Green: Incredible Vibrating Pocket Pussies?

Willie: Yeah, so I put my nose in there, just to see how far in I could get it to go.

Dr. Green: Yes.

Willie: Yeah. But I only got it halfway in, so I take one of them . . .

Dr. Green: Ball-peen hammers?

Willie: Yeah, and I begin hammering away at it and . . .

Dr. Green: Sorry, Willie, you're getting a little too weird for me.

Willie: Yeah, I hate when I do that.

Dr. Green: Hello? You're on the air with Dr. Stanley Green.

Buddy Young, Jr.: Dr. Green, I presume?

Dr. Green: I know this voice.

Buddy: I hope so . . . but let's not use names. But I'm currently appearing at . . . I'm kidding you. Don't get me started on this whole sexual thing. I just want to talk about sex on television.

Dr. Green: That could be very painful.

Buddy: No, not on the TV, Doc. What are you doing, working the room? I'm talking about too much sex on those video cassettes. You can buy them everywhere. My wife came home from the gynecologist. "Honey," she said, "I've got cystitis and *Amadeus*." I said, "Is it serious?" and she said, "Parts of it, but the music is beautiful."

Dr. Green: Buddy, don't call me to try out new material. This isn't Catch a Rising Star. This isn't The Improv.

Buddy: But, seriously, folks, I do have a problem, Dr. Green. I find I'm leaving my hump on stage, if you know what I mean.

Dr. Green: No, I don't know what you mean.

Buddy: Well, when I come off, I can't get a rod.

Dr. Green: A rod?

Buddy: You know, an erection. You're talking to a guy who used to be able to hang wet towels from it.

Dr. Green: I think I see your problem. You're having trouble talking about your peepee. Semantics. Semantics. That's a major problem in sex. It starts in childhood. The boy points at his penis, or maybe, if he's lucky, a girl points at his penis, and he calls it a tinkler or a tickler, and then, as he gets older, and hopefully it gets bigger, he calls it a gristle whistle or a guided muscle, the little man in the firehat or maybe a massive throbbing one-eyed passion snake. But let's call a spade a spade and just say what it really is: The greatest gift God gave us.

Buddy: You're right, Dr. Green. What we need is love today.

Dr. Green: Hello? You're on the air with Dr. Stanley Green.

Penny Lane: Dr. Green? My name is Penny Lane.

Dr. Green: Oh, yes, I've seen you on cable television. You play the piano, right? And have a deep voice? And wear dresses? What seems to be your problem?

Penny: I think you just said it. Dr. Green, I'm a . . . I hate the term transvestite. I prefer to think of myself as someone who can shop in two stores.

Dr. Green: What are you getting at, Penny?

Penny: The problem is, my mother is coming to town, and she doesn't know about me.

Dr. Green: Can I be frank?

Lonely drunk conventioneer (Roy Scheider): "Let's go have a nightcap. Just the two of us."
Penny Lane: "Do you like surprise parties?"

Penny: That's the problem. Should I be Frank? Or should I be Penny when I see my mother. She has no idea.

Dr. Green: Here's a suggestion: Have lunch with her on two successive days. One day, go as Penny. The next day, go as Tom Brokaw, Ted Koppel, anyone. And just say, "Mom, who do you like better? The guy you met today? Or the woman you met yesterday? Mom, didn't you always want to have a daughter?"

Penny: I hope she likes surprise parties.

Dr. Green: Hello? You're on the air with Dr. Stanley Green.

Julius: Dr. Green [cough, cough] . . . Ah-hem! I'm an Orthodox jew. Is it okay to have sex on Yom Kippur?

Dr. Green: Yes, but remember it's a fasting holiday. Hello? You're on the air.

Buddy: Dr. Green, it's me again, babe. Is it all right to fake orgasm during masturbation?

Dr. Green: Oops, we've run out of time. Thanks for calling *On the Air with Dr. Green*.

Buddy: I was only kidding, I was only kidding.

FOURTEEN

≈≈≈≈≈

Other People's Punch Lines— Jabs That Left Me Speechless

On a visit to Israel, where *Soap* aired at midnight on Sundays and was a huge hit, I was walking near the Wailing Wall in Jerusalem when an old man looked at me and said, "Hey, you, hey, fella, hey, Jodie, how's Jessica?"

"She's fine," I said. "She's fine."

"I'll tell you one thing," the old man said. "She's built better than that wall."

• • •

I was pushing a baby carriage one day on the set of *Soap* and slammed a door on my hand and ripped off the top of one finger. Blood spurted everywhere. Somebody wrapped a towel around my hand. Someone else applied a tourniquet to my wrist. Someone else called an ambulance. When the ambulance and a doctor arrived, I realized the top of my finger was missing. "Wait a minute," I said. "Let's find it."

Everyone began studying the floor, like a basketball team hunting for a contact lens.

"I got it," a prop man yelled. "It's in the lock on the door. Look at it. It's there."

The doctor held out a small cup filled with a saline solution. "Give me the top of the finger," the doctor said. "Put it in there."

"I can't," the prop man said. "I can't touch it. I'm props. You need set design."

Once we settled the union jurisdiction, I got into the ambulance, as did the top of my finger, which was floating in the saline solution, and we took off for the hospital at about a million miles an hour. I was in shock, shaking and frightened and queasy, when one of the paramedics flanking me leaned over and said, "You know, man, I'm a studio musician. I've played with Stevie and Marvin Gaye. You think if I sent you tapes, you could listen to them?"

• • •

I was finishing breakfast in a coffee shop in Indianapolis when a woman walked up to me and said, "Are you Billy Crystal?"

"Yes, ma'm," I said.

"I didn't think you were," she said. "I thought he was taller."

• • •

Early in our marriage Janice and I lived directly over the garage in an apartment house in Long Beach. We had a great buy—only $250 a month for four rooms plus access to a sauna—but every five minutes, when the door to the garage went up, our apartment rattled. We were the only young couple in the building.

One day I was sitting in the sauna reading Woody Allen's *Without Feathers,* and just because I was naked, no other reason—I swear, Woody—I got an erection. Just then, an old Jewish man joined me in the sauna. I panicked. I covered my crotch with Woody Allen.

"You new in the building?" the man said.

"Yes," I said.

He said, "Can you come up and fix the hot water?"

117

"I don't work here," I said. "I live here."

"Oh," he said. "Hey, I like Woody Allen. He makes me laugh. Let me see the book."

I still had a hard-on.

"I'm sorry. You can't see the book," I said.

He looked surprised and hurt.

I said, "What the hell? Here's the book."

I was completely exposed. The old man took one look at me and said, "Boy, I've got to get this book."

.　　.　　.

When we were filming *Running Scared* in Chicago, I whacked myself in the head with my pistol one day and split open my nose. Once again, I was whisked off to the hospital, bleeding and in pain. A plastic surgeon stitched me up. I was still groggy when they finally let me leave, and as I strained to sign a release form, an ambulance driver thrust a piece of paper over the form and said, "Just put, 'To Debbie, You look mahvelous.'"

.　　.　　.

Another airport coffee shop. Another morning. Very tired. I reached for my coffee, and a voice said, "Has anyone ever told you you look a lot like Billy Crystal?"

I looked up. "Yes, ma'am," I said. "People tell me that all the time."

"You're not Billy Crystal, are you?"

"No, ma'am."

"Too bad," she said. "You should only have his money."

"Leave your agent at the door."—Comic Relief, *1986.*

FIFTEEN

How Do You Spell Relief? C–O–M–E–D–Y

I always felt *good* doing comedy. I always knew it was what I was supposed to do. But I never felt *important*. Not till I teamed up with Whoopi Goldberg and Robin Williams to host *Comic Relief,* the four-hour minitelethon that, in the spring of 1986, raised money to provide medical supplies and services for the homeless in America.

Maria Shriver asked me on CBS if it wasn't a weird marriage, humor and the homeless, and I said, "No, Ethel Merman and Ernest Borgnine, that was a weird marriage." Comedy often is just the flip side of tragedy. Some people cry when they're happy. Some laugh when they're scared.

The spread of the homeless is enough to scare anyone, to make anyone cry. Of course there are winos and prostitutes, criminals and crazies among the tens of thousands of homeless in America, but there are also mothers and children and men and women who, despite hard work and good intentions, have lost jobs and homes and sometimes hope. "Tell them we're not all bums," a man said to me at a shelter for the homeless in Seattle. Robin put it more eloquently at the House of Ruth in Washington, D.C. He picked up a homeless baby and held the baby in front of the TV cameras and said, "Does this look like a bum?"

Robin may be mildly insane, but he is a sweet, sensitive human being and a comic genius; and Whoopi may be more than slightly raunchy, but she is so quick, so perceptive, and a stunning actress. To collaborate with both of them—planning, writing, promoting, rehearsing and performing *Comic Relief*—was an education and a delight. Whoopi and I worked together for the first time a few weeks earlier, at the Grammy Awards. Thirty minutes before

With Whoopi and Robin.

airtime we decided to switch roles; she'd be me and, with the aid of a wig, I'd be her. "Just one thing," Whoopi said. "When do I say 'mahvelous'?"

"It's simple," I said. "Every time you would normally say 'motherfucker.'"

Trading lines with Robin is, I imagine, like trading forehands with Ivan Lendl from three feet away. No one else comes even close to being so powerful, so explosive. Robin is a Picasso comic. The eye is awry, and the imagery and the ideas are dazzling. And yet Robin is open and receptive. He did a Rambo bit in the *Comic Relief* opening, and he was searching for the best way to connect Southeast Asia to the homeless, so Whoopi said, "The MIAs, Missing in America," and Robin took the line and flew with it.

I loved the idea of the show, and I loved the experience, dozens and dozens of comics contributing time and energy and talent to a good cause. Giants roamed the stage. Legends. Henny Youngman. Jerry Lewis. Steve Allen. Dick Gregory. George Carlin. Gilda Radner. Men and women who had shaped the comedy of the forties and fifties and sixties and seventies. Men and women who had influenced and inspired so many of the younger comics. I just looked at Henny Youngman and his fiddle and I laughed.

Comic Relief reunited Sid Caesar and Carl Reiner, as the Professor and the Interviewer, roles they had played so many times in my childhood, and I got to introduce them. I introduced them simply as two of the reasons I became a comic. I watched most of the acts on TV monitors, but I stood in the wings to watch Sid and Carl. It was like having a catch in Cooperstown with Mickey Mantle.

I knew Carl, but I'd never met Caesar before, and I wanted to say so much to him. I wanted to tell him how my parents used to let me stay up late to watch him. I wanted to tell him about my brothers and me as the Three Haircuts. I wanted to tell him how much I would have given to have been in his writers' room, where Neil Simon and Larry Gelbart and Mel Brooks and Woody Allen and so many other comic wizards fought to get Caesar to use their lines. I wanted to tell him how much I loved his "This Is Your Life" sketch, the one in which little Howard Morris wrapped himself around one of Caesar's legs and clung to him as Caesar stomped about. I wanted to tell him that I used to cling to my father's leg like that when he carried me to bed. I wanted to tell him so much, but all I did was thank him for being with us and for being Sid Caesar.

I tried to go around and thank everyone who took part. I met Madeline Kahn for the first time, and Jon Lovitz of *Saturday Night Live,* and told each of them how brilliant I thought they were. I met Dick Gregory for the first time, and he told me, "You are one entertaining cat." I had never seen so many comics compliment one another's performance without adding, "But you should see the turn I do on that."

I felt so good about doing *Comic Relief.* I felt so good about being a comedian.

And for once, my darlings, it was more important to feel good than to look good.

SIXTEEN

The Comic Eye, the Comic Ear

Sometimes I hear people say things they never said.

Sometimes I see people do things they never did.

I hope you do, too.

Billy Crystal

With my two Wanna-B's, Jennifer (left) and Lindsay Crystal, right before I gave them dimes.